Penny's Plane

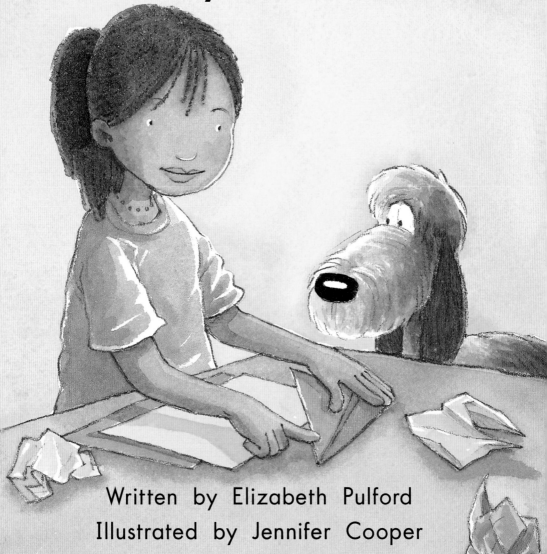

Written by Elizabeth Pulford
Illustrated by Jennifer Cooper

Penny made

a paper plane.

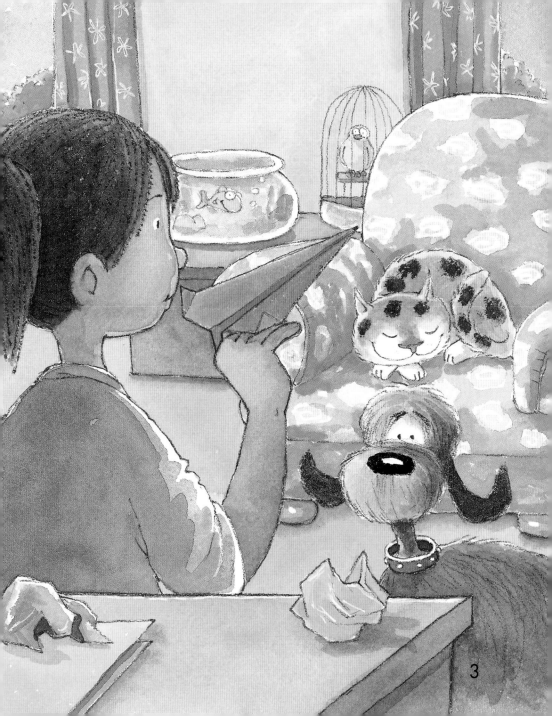

It flew

over the dog.

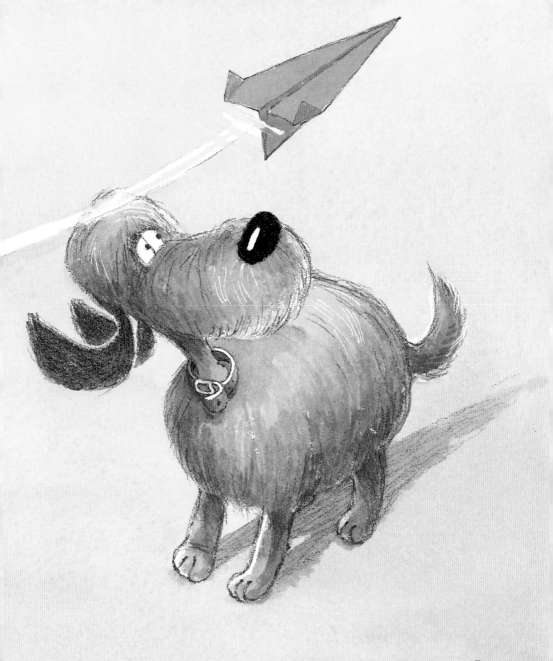

It flew

over the cat.

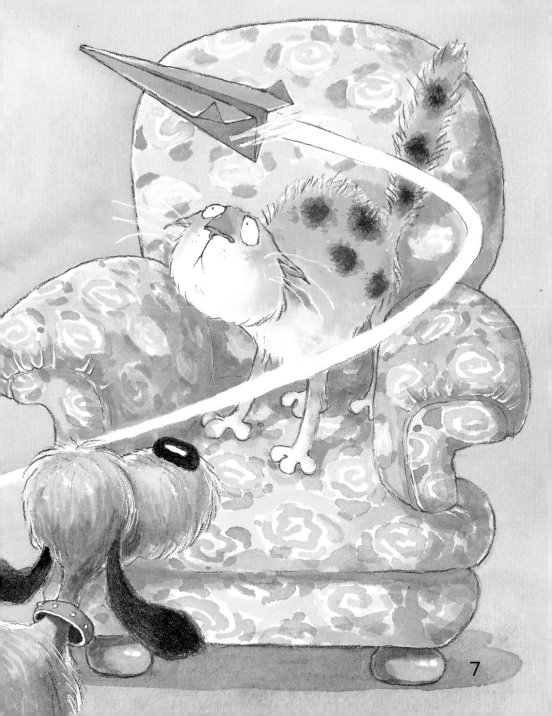

It flew

over the fish.

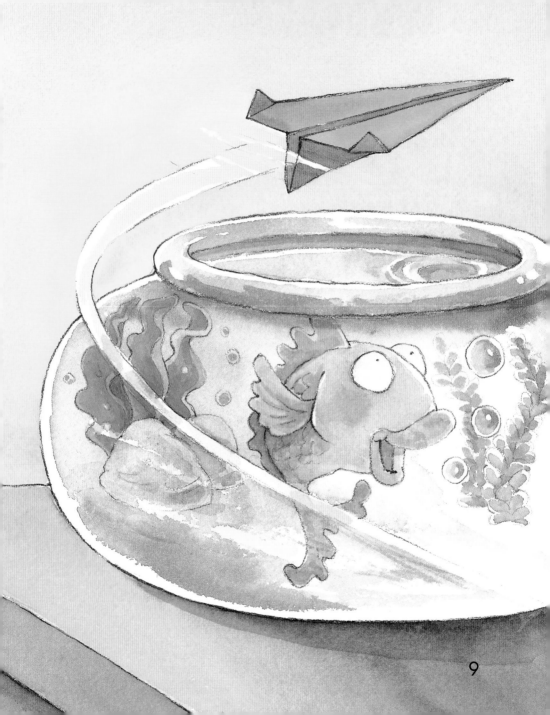

It flew

over the bird.

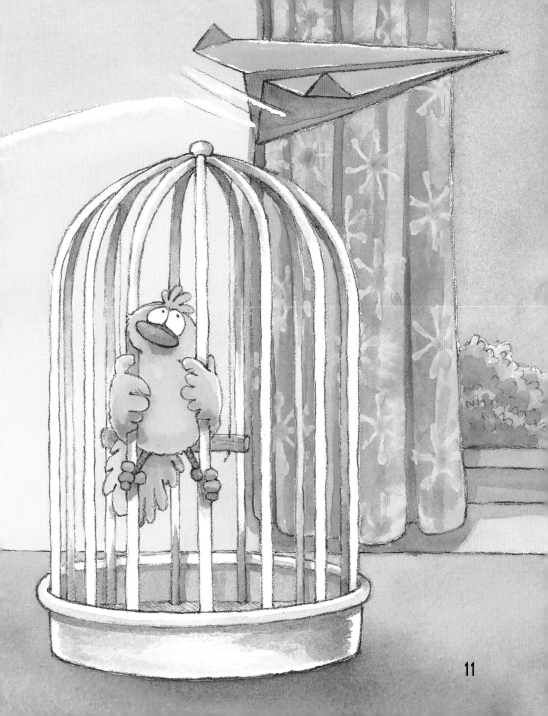

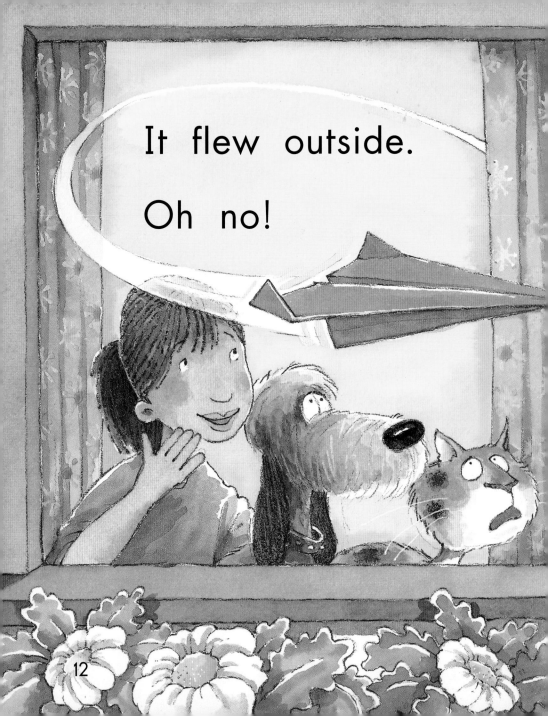